Positive Panda

Written by Shaula Maitland

Illustrated by Kat Stock

For my daughter Nula

Positive Panda © Shaula Maitland, 2019.

Published in the United Kingdom by Calm, Create, Meditate.
A catalogue record of this book is available from the British Library.
First Print: July 2019

Shaula Maitland
www.calmcreatemeditate.com

Illustrated by Kat Stock
www.houseofjack.co.uk

ISBN-978-1-9161643-0-7

You think pandas just munch bamboo all day,

Climb tall trees and hide away.

It may surprise you to learn the truth...

We actually go to school through our youth!

The panda classroom is extremely busy,
It can make our heads feel very dizzy.
But meditation keeps our minds strong,
So we can stay positive all day long.

I'd like to share a Panda secret with you,
So you can learn to have a calm mind too.

When you start to meditate,

It can be hard to concentrate.

First relax from head to toe,

Take deep breaths nice and slow.

A little patience, a little trust,

A quiet room is a must.

Close your eyes, not a peek,

Nice and quiet, not a squeak.

You will visit wonderful places,

And meet lots of friendly faces.

But if for some reason you'd like to wake,

Give your fingers a little shake.

You are safe and always will be,

So come start your journey with me...

Panda's Relaxation

Before meditating, try one of these to help you relax.

Bamboo Soup Breaths

Ask your child to cup their hands to represent Panda's cup of bamboo soup. You want to cool it down. Breathe in through your nose, pause, and breathe out through your mouth, cooling the hot soup. Repeat 3 times.

Panda's Birthday Breaths

Ask your child to imagine they are holding a birthday cake. With each breath in smell the yummy cake. With each breath out blow the pretend candle with one big puff.

Bamboo Leaf Breaths

Lie down and imagine a tiny bamboo leaf on your belly button. With each breath in feel the leaf rise. With each breath out feel the leaf fall. Repeat 3 times. For young children, watching a real leaf rise and fall will help them to focus on their breathing.

Happy Balloon

Close your eyes. Imagine you are holding onto a bright balloon and you're going up, up, high into the sky. Panda is holding onto a balloon next to you. You both fly higher and higher, higher and higher, leaving all of your worries and sadness behind you. As you feel lighter and happier, float down gently to a new place, a happy place. The sun is shining and you are now ready to open your eyes.

Starlight

Close your eyes. Begin to calm your mind. Feel your breaths going in and out, in and out. Imagine Panda is holding a big bright star. The star can be any colour you choose. Look at it shine and glisten in Panda's paws. She holds it out towards you. A beam of starlight glows on your feet, and you feel them completely relax. The starlight slowly moves up your body, relaxing each and every part. It shines on your legs, your bottom and your tummy, all relaxed. The starlight glows gently on your shoulders, your arms, and your hands, all floppy and relaxed. The starlight goes up your neck, reaching the very tip of your head. The warm glow now fills your entire body with beautiful, calm starlight. You are peaceful and still, shining as bright as a star.

Growing Roots

Close your eyes. Push your feet firmly into the ground. Feel your toes start to spread and your feet gently widen. Imagine your feet are growing roots, just like a plant, weaving deep down into the soil. They keep growing, going deeper and deeper, deeper and deeper. You feel strong and steady like a tree.

Panda Hugs

Close your eyes. Imagine Panda is giving you the biggest hug. You feel cosy and warm inside panda's big furry arms. Her soft squeeze feels safe and secure. Everything is going to be just fine.

Let's Meditate!

Guided visualisations are a simple, yet brilliant way to introduce children to meditation. They capture the imagination, therefore making it easier for children to remain focused and enjoy a moment of calm.

Choosing a meditation

The meditations can be read in any order. You may wish to work through sequentially, pick a page at random or choose a theme that suits your child's current learning experiences. You can revisit the scripts as many times as you like. Each time, children will likely follow new story paths, reflecting their current emotions, experiences and thoughts.

Setting up a calm environment

Meditation can be done anywhere: at home, in the classroom or outside. You just need a quiet space. Playing soft relaxation music can help focus the mind and minimise the effects of background noise. Providing a low light source (such as a candle) acts as a visual cue that relaxation is starting.

Reading the Meditations

Allow children time to imagine the scene by reading slowly in a calm, relaxing voice. When you reach a 'Peace Pause' allow children time to meditate freely, exploring the story in silence. The amount of time required will vary for each individual, but will likely lengthen gradually. Always offer the opportunity for children to share their meditations with you afterwards. Meditation fosters emotive discussion and they are likely to have some exciting stories to tell!

Promoting a Positive Mindset

Each script nurtures a positive mindset through gently introducing age-appropriate attitudes and skills, such as perseverance, independence and resilience. They also contain a moment of gratitude. Being thankful encourages children to focus on the positive elements of life.

Panda Symbolism

In meditation, symbolism is very important. Panda appears in all twelve meditations for familiarity. She makes the perfect meditation companion as she is associated with peace, balance, nurture, peaceful determination and gentle strength.

The Green Egg

Patience, Kindness and Responsibility

Close your eyes. Imagine you're sat on a little wooden swing in a beautiful garden. The swing gently rocks from side to side, under a big, tall tree. The leaves shade you from the hot summer sun. You listen as the birds sing you a special song, a song just for you. You feel peaceful and calm.

You decide to explore the garden, following a little grass path. You notice an old, lost toy, nestled among the flowers. You haven't seen that for a while! You go past the sandpit and round the trampoline, until you reach the hedge at the end of the garden.

You look a little closer and see a hole amongst the leaves. A secret passage! You creep through, crunching the leaves beneath your feet. You creep through, ducking under the twisting branches. You creep through, careful not to break any twigs. You look up and spot a splash of black and white ahead. It's Panda!

As you get a little closer you notice that Panda's sat on a bed of twigs, holding an enormous green egg. What could be inside? You hold the egg up to your ear and listen carefully. Full of excitement, you decide to wait for the egg to hatch. You find a comfy branch to sit on and begin the long wait.

You sit, listening to the sounds of the garden. You can hear the next door neighbour mowing the lawn. You can hear the water running gently down the stream. What else can you hear in the garden?

Did you hear a crack? You jump up and take a closer look. The egg is hatching! Purple bubbles flow out of the egg like a mini volcano. Then you see a tiny claw. What's going to be inside? With a great crack the egg pops open and out comes a tiny dragon!

The cute, little dragon smiles, flaps his wings and swishes his tail. He's incredible! You scoop him up into your hands, he's so tiny. How are you going to look after the baby dragon? How will you keep him warm? What will you feed him? What will he drink? Spend some time looking after the little, baby dragon.

Peace Pause

The little dragon yawns and curls up in your arms. You have been so kind to the baby dragon. You have taken great care of him.

Just as he's falling asleep, you hear his mummy calling from outside the hedge. She's come to collect her lost baby! You gently carry him outside. Mummy Dragon lands on the grass in front of you. She thanks you and Panda for looking after her baby so well.

You say goodbye to Baby Dragon. Watch as they fly away together, higher and higher, higher and higher.

The sun is now setting and it's time to go home. You thank Panda for her help. It's been a very busy day. You follow the grass path back to the swing. You sit down to listen for a moment. The garden is so quiet and still. It's been a wonderful day!

It is now time to come back into the room. You notice the sound of my voice getting louder. You can feel the (chair/bed/floor) beneath you. Wiggle your fingers. Wiggle your toes. Rub your tummy. When you are ready, slowly begin to open your eyes.

Midnight Picnic

Sharing, Friendship and Trying Something New

Close your eyes. Imagine you're on holiday with Panda, camping high up a mountain. It's night-time. The stars are twinkling in the sky. The moon is bright and glows softly all around you. The air is clean and fresh. You take a few deep breaths, in and out, in and out.

You hear an owl hooting in the distance and a tiny mouse squeaking goodnight. You sit on a log next to Panda, keeping warm by the fire. Sitting a safe distance away, you watch as the orange flames flicker. Listen to the fire as it crackles and pops. You feel warm and calm.

Panda pulls out a magnificent picnic basket from behind the tent. It's for you to share. She slowly lifts the lid and passes you an unusual fruit. You feel the fruit in your hand. You haven't tried this fruit before. It's good to try new foods. You take a tiny bite. Mmm, it tastes delicious! You sit by the fire, enjoying the picnic together, sharing the most wonderful foods.

Panda starts playing the guitar. She's playing your favourite song. As you start singing together, you notice that more woodland animals come to join you round the fire. They're dancing, singing and having a great time. Spend some time sharing the picnic, enjoying the music with your new friends.

Peace Pause

It's beginning to feel a little chilly. The fire is starting to go out, you need more sticks. You and Panda start searching under some nearby trees. Leaves rustle and crunch beneath your feet. You collect sticks of all shapes and sizes, some big, some small. You keep collecting until your arms are full. Panda helps. When you're ready, you go back to the party and Panda puts some more wood on the fire. You sit down to share the warmth of the fire with your new friends.

Everyone has had lots of fun, but the woodland animals have to go home to bed. They say goodbye, leaving you and Panda alone by the fire. You wrap a soft blanket around you and snuggle up, lovely and warm. You take a moment to enjoy this wonderful night. You look up at the stars sparkling in the sky. The full moon is perfectly round and pure white. As you look up in wonder, a shooting star flashes across the sky. It's time to make a wish. It's the perfect end to a magical night.

Peace Pause

It is now time to come back into the room. You notice the sound of my voice getting louder. You can feel the (chair/bed/floor) beneath you. Wiggle your fingers. Wiggle your toes. Rub your tummy. When you are ready, slowly begin to open your eyes.

On the Farm

Creativity, Resilience, Perseverance and Independence

Close your eyes. Imagine you're on a farm. You're stood in a muddy yard next to a big, wooden barn. Your boots squelch and slide with every step, leaving a trail of footprints in the mud behind you. You can hear the cows mooing, the pigs snorting and the chickens clucking with glee. It's a new day, a new beginning, a fresh start.

You have the best idea! You are going to make a den, but not just any den – a castle! But how are you going to make it? You spot a large pile of wood in the corner of the yard that might be useful. You climb over a fence into an empty field and begin searching for the perfect tree. The long grass swishes and sways in the breeze. The sky grows darker and light raindrops begin to fall. You search and search and search some more. You search by the river, you search by the duck pond and you even search by the old, muddy tractor, but you can't find the perfect tree. Feeling a little disappointed, you head back to the yard. You'll have to find another way.

The wind is getting stronger and the rain is getting heavier. You dive into the barn for some cover. You take off your wet raincoat and give it a shake. Water droplets fly off in all directions.

You sit down on a hay bale. It feels scratchy on the back of your legs. You twiddle the hay between your fingers for a moment. How are you going to build a castle?

Your tummy begins to rumble. It's time for lunch. You open your bag and find the best sandwich ever. It's your favourite filling, a sandwich just for you. You munch away happily.

Then you have an idea. You could use the hay bales in the barn to make a castle. You could stack them up like bricks, higher and higher. You feel excited. You've never made a castle before. Spend some time on your own, building your castle.

Peace Pause

You hear a quiet creek at the door. It's Panda. She's come to see if you need any help. It's your choice, you can build the castle on your own or you can ask Panda to help. When you've finished, enjoy playing in your wonderful castle.

Peace Pause

The sun is setting and the barn is getting darker. It's time to go home. You step back and admire your castle, it's wonderful! The hay bales are stacked high, safe and strong. You thank Panda for playing; it's been so much fun.

It is now time to come back into the room. You notice the sound of my voice getting louder. You can feel the (chair/bed/floor) beneath you. Wiggle your fingers. Wiggle your toes. Rub your tummy. When you are ready, slowly begin to open your eyes.

Mermaid Cave

Curiosity, Courage, Awe and Wonder

Close your eyes. Imagine you're with Panda, swimming in a cool, refreshing pool of water. A powerful waterfall creates a curtain of water, crashing down on the rocks below. It glistens like a rainbow in the sunlight. Enchanted by its magic, you swim closer. You wonder if the stories are true. Do mermaids live behind this beautiful waterfall? Curious, you decide to find out for yourself.

You bravely jump through the powerful flow of water, only to find the entrance to a damp, gloomy cave. Panda hands you a burning torch to light your way. As you step deeper into the cave, the ground is wet and slippery. You step carefully and slowly, edging deeper and deeper, deeper and deeper. You are careful. You are brave. You are safe.

A few more steps and the cave opens up to a magical new world. The purple trees are abundant with juicy fruits and colourful birds. The lake is glittery pink and perfectly still. Wow! You have come to the most wonderful place. Spend a moment enjoying this amazing new place.

Panda touches your shoulder and points. There, hiding behind a giant rock, is the most beautiful mermaid. Her hair waves gently in the breeze and the scales on her tail glisten in the sun. The mermaid smiles and gracefully swims over to say hello. She's very friendly. Spend some time getting to know her and enjoying this magical place.

Peace Pause

The mermaid leads you back to the cave entrance. You say goodbye to your new friend and thank her for showing you her beautiful home. She dives back into the pink, glittery pool.

You hold Panda's paw. It feels so soft. You carefully make your way back through the cave, feeling the wet, cold stone under your soft, bare feet. You can hear the waterfall in the distance. You can hear the crashing water getting louder and louder, as you get closer and closer, closer and closer. You made it! There in front of you is the most powerful, wonderful waterfall. What colour is the water? You dive through the waterfall and into the refreshing pool where you started. You float like a star, bobbing around peacefully.

It is now time to come back into the room. You notice the sound of my voice getting louder. You can feel the (chair/bed/floor) beneath you. Wiggle your fingers. Wiggle your toes. Rub your tummy. When you are ready, slowly begin to open your eyes.

Birthday Surprise

Teamwork, Kindness and Friendship

Close your eyes. Imagine you're walking through the jungle. The sun glimmers through the leafy canopy above. The fallen leaves are a soft carpet beneath your feet. You gently push through a curtain of leafy vines, until you reach a clearing. In the middle of the jungle, in the middle of the clearing, is a large and very old meeting stone. Standing beside it are your friends: Tiger, Monkey and Bear. You have come together to plan a birthday surprise for Panda. Panda is always so kind; it will be nice to surprise her. Tiger will make a card. Monkey will find a table and some balloons. Bear will bring drinks and party food. You choose to make a birthday cake.

You go to the jungle kitchen and get a big bowl. You start by mixing the flour, sugar, eggs and butter. You mix it round and round, round and round. Panda is going to love it! What sort of cake is it going to be? You pop it in the oven. How will you decorate it?

Once the cake is ready, you head back to the meeting stone. Your friends are waiting for you. The table looks wonderful! The balloons are up, the food is ready, but there's just one big space left to fill! You place your finished cake carefully down on the table. You feel very proud.

You hear the crinkle of leaves; it's Panda, she's coming! You all hide quietly behind a tree, ready to surprise her. You lean into the tree so that you can't be seen. Feel the rough tree trunk against your body. You are all as quiet as can be. You are so quiet you can hear your breaths going in and out, in and out.

As Panda comes through the bushes, you all jump out shouting, "Surprise!" Panda jumps and grins! She is so happy! You all sit down at the table. Panda cuts the cake and you all enjoy a slice. Notice how happy everyone is. Spend some time enjoying the party. Perhaps you'll play some party games.

Peace Pause

Everyone's had a great time. Panda thanks you again. She is so grateful to have such kind friends. You are all very sleepy after such a busy day.

It is now time to come back into the room. You notice the sound of my voice getting louder. You can feel the (chair/bed/floor) beneath you. Wiggle your fingers. Wiggle your toes. Rub your tummy. When you are ready, slowly begin to open your eyes.

Crystal River

Individuality and Requesting Help

Close your eyes. Imagine you're wearing the brightest, yellow welly boots you have ever seen. Water trickles over them gently, as you stand in the middle of a shallow river. The water is clean and clear. Press your boots into the ground below, feeling strong and steady. Watch as two friendly fish chase each other playfully in the water.

The river ripples softly over a collection of crystals that glisten and shine under the water like jewels. Then you see it. Each crystal is different, each unique in its own way. They are all different colours, shapes and sizes. They are all beautiful.

Then you see Panda. She is stood on a little bridge above the river. She's wearing her wellies too! She loves crystals. She tells you that this is a magic river. All the crystals have super-powers. They can all do different things and are equally special.

Ask the crystals for help and watch as one lights up. Pick it up. Hold it tight. The crystal will show you its super-power.

Peace Pause

The crystal will carry on helping for as long as you need. Thank the crystal. What would you like to do with the crystal? Would you like to put it back in the river or keep it in your pocket?

Panda helps you climb up and out of the river. You sit together on the bridge with your legs dangling down over the river. You can talk to Panda and she will listen. You can tell her anything at all.

Peace Pause

You give Panda a big hug and say goodbye. She smiles and gives you a flower from behind her ear.

It is now time to come back into the room. You notice the sound of my voice getting louder. You can feel the (chair/bed/floor) beneath you. Wiggle your fingers. Wiggle your toes. Rub your tummy. When you are ready, slowly begin to open your eyes.

Beach Day

Independence and Self-belief

Close your eyes. Imagine you're on a lovely, sunny beach. Push your feet down into the warm, soft sand. Feel it between your toes. You can hear the waves gently crashing against the rocks, the seagulls high above you in the sky and the happy song of the ice cream van. You're feeling happy. Today is going to be a great day!

You walk along the beach looking for the perfect spot to build a sandcastle. You have built them before with other people. This time you would like to build one all by yourself, with no help whatsoever. You have so many ideas. You want to build it just the way you imagined, all the way up, high into the sky. You know you can do it! You set to work; wetting the sand, filling your bucket and stacking, one by one. The sandcastle is getting taller and taller, taller and taller. You have to reach up high to add another bucket. You are very careful not to knock it over. Spend some time building your sandcastle just the way you want it.

Peace Pause

The sun is now setting. You have been building for a long time. Your sandcastle is looking fantastic! You stand back and admire it. You're feeling very proud. You built the best sandcastle and you did it all by yourself.

Looking out to sea, you notice Panda rowing towards you in a little green boat. She rides the waves, landing on the beach in front of you. It's great to see her! She leans over and hands you a tiny flag; the perfect finishing touch. You thank Panda and add it to the top of your sandcastle.

It is now time to come back into the room. You notice the sound of my voice getting louder. You can feel the (chair/bed/floor) beneath you. Wiggle your fingers. Wiggle your toes. Rub your tummy. When you are ready, slowly begin to open your eyes.

Out at Sea

Courage, Patience, Awe and Wonder

Close your eyes. Imagine you're out at sea in a little wooden boat. The white sail sways gently against the bright blue sky. The waves calmly bob you up and down, up and down, up and down. Panda is sat with her feet dangled over the side. You join her, feeling the cold water swash against your toes.

Panda hands you an ice cream. What flavour is it? Does it have sprinkles? It's starting to melt. Cold ice cream drips slowly down the cone, making your hands sticky. You quickly lick the top. It's yummy! Enjoy the refreshing taste, watching the waves for a moment.

Peace Pause

Panda points excitedly and out jumps the most beautiful dolphin. It twists and dives, swimming happily in the water next to the boat. You can't believe your eyes! What an incredible moment! The friendly dolphin comes up to your feet and nudges them, wanting to play. It smiles and asks you if you would like a ride!

Feeling brave, you hop onto Dolphin's back. She will look after you. Dolphin begins to swim, taking you for an exciting ride. Feel the cold sea rush over your body. Taste the salt on your lips. Dolphin jumps in and out of the water, in and out, in and out. She asks you where you would like to go. Spend some time with dolphin, enjoying the ride and exploring the sea.

Peace Pause

Dolphin swims back to the little wooden boat where Panda is waiting for you. You climb the little ladder and are safely back on board. Panda passes you a big, soft towel. You wrap it tightly around you, feeling warm and snug.

You thank Dolphin for an amazing ride in the sea. Dolphin dives down into the water and brings up a tiny box. She squeaks and clicks, telling you not to open it until you reach the shore. Look carefully at the box. How big is it? How heavy is it? You want to open it straight away, but you'll wait, just like Dolphin asked.

The sails swish round and the wind picks up as you head towards the shore. Panda glides the boat across the water, so smooth and calm. You wash gently up onto the shore and step out onto the warm, sandy beach.

You look at the box once again. What could be inside? You give it a little shake, rattling it next to your ear. Slowly you open it, taking a peek inside. It's a shell, the perfect keepsake from your special day at sea. You lift the shell to your ear to hear the waves, and perhaps even Dolphin in the distance. Now you can always remember your time at sea.

It is now time to come back into the room. You notice the sound of my voice getting louder. You can feel the (chair/bed/floor) beneath you. Wiggle your fingers. Wiggle your toes. Rub your tummy. When you are ready, slowly begin to open your eyes.

Rainbow Slide

Turn Taking, Courage and Self-Belief

Close your eyes. Imagine you're at the park, climbing up steps to the coolest, biggest slide you have ever seen. The slide twists and turns down a big hill. It's so high; you can't even see the bottom. Panda is at the top, waiting for her turn. You join the queue. Sometimes waiting is tricky, it can feel like a long time when you're excited. Finally, it's Panda's turn. She sits down carefully and pushes herself off the edge. She's very brave. Wheeee! It sounds like lots of fun!

Finally it's your turn. You take a few steps forward and sit at the top of the slide. Your tummy flutters and you feel a little nervous. That can sometimes happen when you try something new. You take a few minutes to look around. You're feeling brave. You can do this!

Suddenly the slide turns to a fabulous rainbow. The colours are magnificent. As you slide down, you go through a tunnel of colour. Each colour is special in its own way. Feel the colour go through your body, as if it was being coloured in with a giant paintbrush.

'Peace Pause' after each colour

The slide changes to a deep shade of red. I feel energetic.

The slide turns a bright shade of orange. I am creative.

The slide turns a fresh shade of yellow. I feel happy.

The slide turns a lush shade of green. I like to try new things.

The slide turns a soft shade of pink. I am loved.

The slide turns a calm shade of blue. I tell the truth.

The slide turns a rich shade of purple. I understand.

You are now at the bottom of the slide. Thank the rainbow slide for the wonderful journey of colour. It has been a wonderful day at the park.

It is now time to come back into the room. You notice the sound of my voice getting louder. You can feel the (chair/bed/floor) beneath you. Wiggle your fingers. Wiggle your toes. Rub your tummy. When you are ready, slowly begin to open your eyes.

Flower Fairy

Curiosity and Requesting Help

Close your eyes. Imagine you're sat down, leaning back against a big, green tree. The sunlight flashes through the leaves, displaying beautiful shades of green. Panda is asleep next to you, snoring loudly. Her lips wobble as she snuffles and snorts. You take a big, deep breath, filling your lungs with the cool, crisp air.

As you rest in the forest, under the big tree, you notice a colourful butterfly fluttering close to some flowers. You follow it, taking a closer look. One flower stands tall, high above all the rest. There's something special about this flower. All of its petals are closed, like a new little bud waiting to bloom. What colour is your flower? How big is it?

One by one the petals begin to open. Watch as each petal unfolds. Inside, curled asleep, is a tiny fairy, a flower fairy! The fairy slowly begins to wake up. It yawns and stretches its arms wide and tall. She looks up and smiles, glad to see you. The fairy wants to be your friend. She has been waiting for you to find her. Questions begin bubbling in your mind. You have so many lovely things to ask. Spend time chatting to your fairy, asking her lots of questions.

Peace Pause

Your fairy asks if you would like any help. Is there something that you are finding tricky at the moment? Tell your fairy and she will do her best to help you.

Peace Pause

It is now time to say goodbye to your fairy. Panda has come to walk you back to the big, green tree. You thank your fairy for listening and begin to walk back, holding Panda's paw. You sit down and lean back against the strong tree trunk.

It is now time to come back into the room. You notice the sound of my voice getting louder. You can feel the (chair/bed/floor) beneath you. Wiggle your fingers. Wiggle your toes. Rub your tummy. When you are ready, slowly begin to open your eyes.

The Only Cloud

Perseverance, Curiosity and Pride

Close your eyes. Imagine you're at school, playing on the field. The sun is high in the sky, beaming down. It's lucky that you're wearing your sun hat. There are children playing football, children doing handstands and children playing chase. Everyone's having lots of fun. You lay down on the warm, freshly cut grass. You lay there for a moment, looking up at the blue sky. There's just one cloud, fluffy and white. Watch as it changes shape. What does the cloud look like?

After some time, you make your way to the climbing tree. It's a tall, old tree in the corner of the field. It's the best climbing tree in the field with lots of low branches. When you arrive, you feel the rough bark with your hand. You look up at the bright green leaves above.

You whisper quietly, asking the tree if you can climb it. Magically, the tree changes colour. Little wooden steps begin to come out from the trunk, one by one, a step at a time. See the steps appearing, going up and up the tree like a spiral. Going round and round, up and up, higher and higher. What's at the top? You take your first step onto the tree's staircase. Each step is wide and strong, you are perfectly safe. You begin to climb the stairs, higher and higher, higher and higher.

Peace Pause

You've been climbing for a long time now. You have been working very hard to get to the top. You haven't given up. You've carried on trying even though it's taking a long time. You sit down on a step, taking a well-earned rest. Have a long, cold drink from your water bottle and look down at the field below. The children are still playing and having fun.

You take a few more steps. At the top is the white, fluffy cloud you were looking at earlier. Panda is standing on top waiting for you. She holds her paw out and helps you jump across. The cloud is bouncy. You spring up and down as if you were on a big bouncy castle! Panda wants to show you around this magical cloud. Spend some time exploring.

Peace Pause

You thank Panda for showing you such a beautiful place. You have never visited a cloud before. You feel very proud that you reached the top.

You slowly make your way back to the tree steps. But to your surprise they have changed. It is now a slide, a big curly slide and it looks like lots of fun! You sit down, say goodbye to Panda and begin to slide down. You control how fast you come down. You can go as fast or as slow as you like, going down, down, down all the way to the bottom. You curl, round and round the wise, old tree, all the way to the bottom. You are now back in the school field, just in time for the bell.

It is now time to come back into the room. You notice the sound of my voice getting louder. You can feel the (chair/bed/floor) beneath you. Wiggle your fingers. Wiggle your toes. Rub your tummy. When you are ready, slowly begin to open your eyes.

White Box

Creativity and Pride

Close your eyes. Imagine you're in a white room filled with nothing. No table. No door. No window. You are stood in a big box of white. The walls are asking for colour.

In your hand is a long, thin paintbrush. You look around for some paint. There's no paint. Unsure, you walk over to the blank white wall and place the brush softly against it. To your surprise a big splash of colour appears in front of you. You try again and another splash of colour appears. You begin to fill the blank walls with colour, experimenting and feeling more and more confident with every brushstroke. In no time at all, you are painting the most wonderful paintings. Spend time noticing the colours and pictures that appear.

Peace Pause

Your white box is now filled with an array of colour. You stand proudly in the middle and admire your paintings. You thank the paintbrush for allowing you to colour.

A door appears in the corner of the room. Panda has come to see your amazing paintings. You proudly show her your colourful room. Panda loves your paintings and shows you her favourite. Well done. You have created something beautiful!

It is now time to come back into the room. You notice the sound of my voice getting louder. You can feel the (chair/bed/floor) beneath you. Wiggle your fingers. Wiggle your toes. Rub your tummy. When you are ready, slowly begin to open your eyes.

Made in the USA
Middletown, DE
11 February 2022